"I was born in London in 1946 and grew up in a sweet shop in Essex. For several years I worked as a graphic designer, but in 1980 I decided to concentrate on writing and illustrating books for children.

My wife, Annette, and I have two grown-up children, Ben and Amanda, and we have put down roots in Suffolk.

I haven't recently counted how many books there are with my name on the cover but Percy the Park Keeper accounts for a good many of them. I'm reliably informed that they have sold more than three million copies. Hooray!

I didn't realise this when I invented Percy, but I can now see that he's very like my mum's dad, my grandpa. I even have a picture of him giving a ride to my brother and me in his old home-made wooden wheelbarrow!"

NICK BUTTERWORTH

PERCY'S FRIEND
THE FOX

NICK BUTTERWORTH

HarperCollins *Children's Books*

Thanks Graham Daldry. You're a wizard.

Thanks Atholl McDonald. You're a hero!

First published in Great Britain by HarperCollins Publishers Ltd in 2001

ISBN-13: 978 0 00 778249 9

ISBN-10: 0 00 778249 7

Text and illustrations copyright © Nick Butterworth 2001

The author asserts the moral right to be identified as the author of the work.

Visit our website at: www.harpercollinschildrensbooks.co.uk

Printed and bound in Belgium

MY FRIEND THE FOX

Some foxes can be sneaky, but not this one. He's very friendly and he's funny too, usually when he doesn't mean to be!

He says he can read but I do wonder about that because he often holds the book upside down. Then he'll start reading in a peculiar, low voice. "Grrworr ffss hhee-hhee grrrwll pipipip ffss grrhoo..."

He says it's a special way of speaking that only foxes understand.

Once, when he came to stay for the night in my hut, he said he thought his feet were sticking out of bed, so he got out to have a look.

"It's alright," he said. "They weren't."

Some of my friends may
not agree with me, but I
really think the fox is very
musical. I don't know
anyone else who could play
Jingle Bells on the icicles.
I know a bit about music (I play the
accordion) and I think it must be
very hard to play anything at all
on the icicles, especially when
some of your best notes keep
breaking off.

THE FOX REALLY LIKES . . .

Giving presents. I'm afraid he's not very
good at wrapping them, but he tries hard.

Climbing. He's particularly good at *Up*.
He is not quite so good at *Down*.

THE FOX DOESN'T LIKE . . .

Hide-and-seek. For some strange reason, he always seems to be the first to be found.

Shadows. Not if they're not his own.
Not at night, anyway.

Just once or twice, the fox
has come knocking on my
door because he has had a
bad dream. But this one
wasn't a bad dream at all.
He told me he'd had
a dream about a
picnic tree.

He must have gone to bed feeling hungry!
He said that there were all sorts of things
to eat hanging from the branches.
    Even the spaces between some of the
branches made the shapes of picnic food,
                but that wasn't so good
                    because you can't
                        eat spaces.

I've got lots of pictures in my photo album.

When the fox came to a fancy dress party, he wore a fancy dress!

The fox always enjoys a game of conkers.

Here are some I took of my good friend, the fox.

The fox in his cardboard boat. Luckily, the pond isn't very deep.

This is actually a picture of me taken by the fox. Well, it was supposed to be anyway.

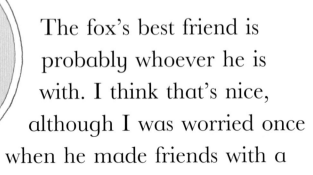

The fox's best friend is probably whoever he is with. I think that's nice, although I was worried once when he made friends with a snowman. I thought he would be upset when the snowman melted.

He was a bit, but not for long. He said that's what snowmen do and they don't mind. Do you know, I think the fox was right.

STARRY-EYED FOX

The sky looks very beautiful,
The stars look very nice.
Like a dark blue tablecloth,
With little bits of rice.

Those stars are called The Plough, I think,
And there's Orion's Belt.
Are those Orion's Trousers?
They're made of dark blue felt.

There's a funny thing with stars;
Although they seem quite bright,
They're only teeny-tiny, so
They don't give out much light.

If you really concentrate,
You'll see a shooting star.
You have to watch quite carefully;
They don't shoot very far.

The sky at night is very strange.
It's close and far away.
It just goes on for ever and ever
And ever and ever and ever and ever and ever and ever and ever and ever and ever and ever

FAVOURITE PLACES

One of the fox's favourite places is one of
mine, too. On a sunny afternoon he likes
nothing better than to snooze lazily in a
hammock.

I put this hammock up for myself, but I
had to leave it to sort out a little problem for
the mice. When I came back, there was the
fox! He said that he had found the hammock
empty, and as nobody seemed to want it, it
was a shame to waste it.

When he's feeling more energetic, you will sometimes find the fox playing by the bandstand. There's a statue of a horse nearby. When he thinks nobody is looking, the fox will jump on the horse's back and pretend to go for a ride.

Perhaps the fox's favourite place of all is his home in the tree house. It's one of my favourite places, too, because I know that's where I'll find my friend the fox!

Here he is, outside his own front door.
The fox is full of fun, usually smiling
and he's always pleased to see you.